BWD,
Essex Works.
of life

D0754939

BOY

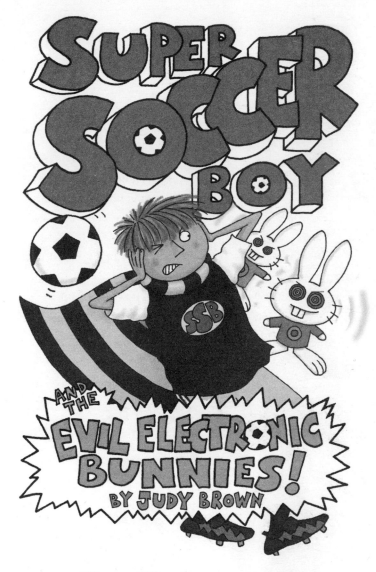

Piccadilly Press • London

For Alan

First published in Great Britain in 2010 by
Piccadilly Press Ltd, 5 Castle Road, London NW1 8PR
www.piccadillypress.co.uk

ISBN: 978 1 84812 053 2

1 3 5 7 9 10 8 6 4 2

Printed in the UK by CPI Bookmarque, Croydon, CR0 4TD
Cover design by Simon Davis
Cover illustration by Judy Brown
Text design by Simon Davis

Chapter One

A Very Bunny Birthday

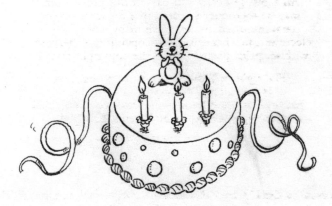

Harry Gribble, also known as Super Soccer Boy, was walking home from school with his best mate Jake. Lots of people greeted him on the way — ever since the huge thunderstorm that had transformed him from 'Harry Gribble who couldn't even dribble' into the super-powered, super-football player he was today, Harry had become a bit of a celebrity.

'Coming to the park for a kickabout?' asked Jake.

This was another way that Harry's life had changed. These days people were falling over themselves just for the opportunity to play football with him instead of avoiding him like the plague. Not only that, they actually *wanted* to be on his team.

'Sorry, I can't,' said Harry, disappointed. 'It's Daisy's birthday. I have to go straight home for her special birthday tea – her friends from

nursery are coming and they all want to meet me.' Harry blushed. 'Hey, why don't you come too?' he added enthusiastically. 'It'll be much less boring if you're there.'

'Er, no offence, Harry, but spending my afternoon with a bunch of two- and three-year-olds is *not* my idea of fun.'

'Nor mine,' groaned Harry, trudging off.

Harry turned the corner of Crumbly Drive and tried to get himself into a party mood. As much as his little sister irritated him, he didn't want to spoil her birthday by being a party pooper. So by the time he reached the front door, he'd managed to fix his best attempt at a cheesy Happy Birthday grin to his face.

'HARRY!' Daisy virtually exploded when he came through the door. She threw herself straight at him, hugged him tight and covered

him with jammy fingerprints and sticky kisses.
'Look at me, Harry, I'm a *bunny*!'

Daisy was *totally* obsessed with bunnies. She
had bunny slippers, bunny wallpaper, bunny
T-shirts, bunny pyjamas, bunnies on her duvet
cover, several toy bunnies, a bunny-shaped night
light and so on and so on. Now, she was dressed

as a bunny as well, complete with fluffy white tail and big floppy ears.

'Doesn't she look adorable!' said Harry's mum. 'One of her friends from nursery got it for her. She's so thrilled!' Harry could see that his mum was going all gooey and was on the verge of mumsy tears. You know the sort.

'Er, yes, she looks very cute,' said Harry, trying to wipe off the jam that Daisy had deposited on his trousers. 'I think I'd better go and change.'

'Good idea. And while you're up there you can write your name on the gift tag for Daisy's present from all of us. It's in our room on the chest of drawers. When Dad gets home we can give it to her.'

Mum opened the door to the living room, which was full of toddlers and a

collection of mums and dads. Harry got a brief blast of deafening squeals and a glimpse of the total mayhem inside before she shut the door behind her.

'Hi, Ron!' said Harry to his pet rat as he went into his room. He chucked his school bag on the floor and took Ron out of his cage. 'I'd better not take you downstairs, they'd totally freak.' He chuckled, imagining the effect his rat would have on a room full of toddlers . . . and their mums.

Harry changed his clothes and was just wondering how long he could hang around in his room before he was missed when he heard Daisy's sing-song voice calling upstairs.

'Harry! Harry! Haaarrryyyy! Come and play. Come and play stachooos.'

'Oh no!' said Harry to Ron. 'Won't be long, Daisy!' he called back. 'Just got to do something for Mum.'

Harry went into his parents' room where Daisy's present – wrapped in bunny paper – sat waiting for him. He knew what it was of course – it was

yet another bunny. But this
was no ordinary bunny – it
was the latest 'must have' toy.
If you were three years old,
that was. It was an interactive
electronic bunny!

Everyone at nursery
had one already –
at least that was
what Daisy kept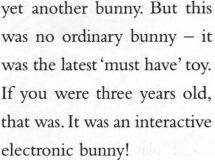
saying. They were being advertised everywhere
non-stop, with the most annoying jingle you
have ever heard. The kind that gets into your
head, gets stuck there and drives you nuts:

You'll love your little bunny
He makes every day feel sunny.
He's so sweet and he's so funny.
He's your bunny, bunny, bunny, bunny love . . .

'Yuk!' said Harry as the tune went round and
round in his brain.

Harry jumped downstairs in one super leap
and cart-wheeled across the hall – not because

he was in a hurry to join the party, but just because he could. He took a deep breath and opened the door to the living room.

'HARRY!'

Earsplitting toddler shrieks erupted as he went in and what felt like hundreds of sticky toddler fingers pulled him into the middle of the room. The mums and dads looked at him admiringly and nudged each other.

Out of the corner of his eye, Harry spotted an

electronic bunny, presumably brought along by one of Daisy's friends. He could have sworn it was looking at him when it suddenly burst into life and started singing the bunny jingle. Harry's little hangers-on dragged him towards it and danced around him, joining in with the song.

'. . . *bunny, bunny, bunny, bunny loooooove.*'

A shiver went down Harry's spine.

'That is truly creepy,' he said.

Chapter Two

Sixth Sense?

Three games of musical bumps, one of musical statues, one of pin-the-tail-on-the-rabbit and a pass-the-parcel later, it was time for Daisy's friends to go home.

'Bye, bye, everybunny!' giggled Daisy as she handed out the party bags.

'Thanks for coming,' said Mum, looking exhausted.

It was at this point that Harry's dad came down the garden path and Harry had a sneaking suspicion that he'd been waiting outside all this time.

'Is it safe now?' he whispered to Harry as he waved goodbye to Daisy's friends who were by now quite tired and a lot quieter.

'DADDY!' said Daisy, still seemingly full of energy. She was like that – she'd bounce off the  walls for hours and then suddenly fall asleep, sometimes into her dinner. 'Can I have my bunny now please?' she asked, beaming. They all knew that Daisy was smart enough to work out that, since it was the only thing she'd actually asked for, she was pretty sure she'd get one.

'Bunny?' said Mum, pretending quite convincingly not to know what she was on about.

A flash of sheer panic and desperate disappointment crossed Daisy's face. She was a millisecond away from blubbing.

'Oh yes,' Mum added quickly, before disaster struck. 'There is one more present upstairs, I think. Harry, could you pop up and get it please?'

'That was a close one,' whispered Dad.

Harry whizzed upstairs, dashed into his room briefly to pick up Ron, then collected the present wrapped in its bunny

paper. He returned to the living room and before you could say 'Electronic bunny', Daisy had ripped off the paper and was hugging the box.

'Shall we take it out, Daisy, so that we can see what it does?' asked Dad.

'Love my bunny, bunny, bunny, bunny,' said Daisy emotionally.

'Yes, sweety, we know,' said Mum, going all gooey again.

Harry stared at the bunny in the box and got another weird shiver. 'Those things *really* give me the creeps,' he said.

'Well, I would hardly expect someone obsessed with football to be interested in an electronic bunny,' Mum said defensively. 'I think they're cute.'

Daisy poked her tongue out at Harry.

He decided to leave them to it and went into the kitchen.

Harry sat Ron on the kitchen table and put on the TV.

'. . . and the mysterious crime wave continues,' said the newsreader. 'Bob, is there any more you can tell us?'

'Well, Samantha, it's all, as you say, quite mysterious. There has been a *massive* increase in burglaries across the entire country in the last six weeks. Police tell us they have nothing to go on.'

'Someone must have stolen their toilets,' laughed Harry.

Ron looked unimpressed.

'You know – nothing to *go* on! Yes, I know it's an old joke but it's still funny,' Harry said.

'Things have really escalated in the last couple of days,' continued the reporter, 'and police advice is that we should all make sure that doors and windows are shut and locked, especially at night. I talked to one of the most recent burglary victims . . .'

Harry looked at the TV. The reporter was interviewing a member of the public in their now fairly empty front room.

'I can't even get away from the stupid bunnies out here. Look, Ron, they've got one too. They are sooo annoying,' moaned Harry.

'Harry, come and see what this thing can do,' called Dad. 'It's amazing!'

Harry sighed, turned off the TV and picked up Ron who was tucking in to a piece of birthday cake.

'Coming,' he said.

Chapter Three

Bunny Suspicions

Harry had a restless night. First, he dreamed that he was being chased by a giant bunny. After that, he dreamed that all their doors and windows were open and someone had come in and stolen his football posters, programmes, statistic books and the football that they gave him as a special gift at the F.A. Cup Final. He woke up feeling groggy and out of sorts, dragged himself to the bathroom, got washed and dressed and headed downstairs for breakfast.

Mum and Dad were already up and watching the breakfast news.

'I don't know what this country's coming to,' said his mum. 'When I was a girl you could go out without having to lock anything up. It's criminal.'

'Very funny, dear!' said his dad.

'I wasn't trying to be funny,' she said.

'Oh . . . sorry. Morning, Harry.'

'They're still talking about the crime wave then?' Harry asked.

'Yes, there's a news special on this morning.'

Harry grabbed some cereal and sat in front of the TV. A local news reporter was standing in the hall of a house that had been burgled the night before.

'Those blasted bunnies are everywhere,' said Harry, spotting another bunny like Daisy's by the front door of the house.

'Oh yes,' said Mum. 'Isn't that funny?'

'Just freaky, if you ask me,' he said.

'This morning,' said the reporter, 'there were over one hundred burglaries reported in this district alone. But the strangest thing,' he said, pausing dramatically and leaning into the camera, 'is that they all have one thing in common. No

evidence!' Harry was intrigued. 'There are no signs of a break in, no fingerprints, and it seems that these burglars manage to lock the doors behind them when they leave. In a moment we will be talking to Mrs Perry, a mother of two small boys, and another victim of these fiendish burglars.'

'It says in the paper that some people have been burgled several times,' added Dad. 'I blame the government.'

'I blame the government!' said a weepy Mrs Perry. 'There should be more policemen on the streets.'

'Tell us exactly what happened,' said the reporter, putting on his most serious expression and shoving the microphone into her face.

The woman was standing with her children. They were looking very sorry for themselves. Next to them was a gaping hole where there had obviously been a large TV. Various electrical leads were strewn on the floor.

'It's just awful. I came down this morning and it was all gone. The plasma TV, Play-Station, Xbox, the Wii, even my husband's laptop. I just . . .'

But Harry had stopped listening. He jumped to his feet spilling half of his cereal on to the table. Ron dived in.

'LOOK!' Harry shouted, pointing at the TV.

'What on earth is it, Harry?' said Dad.

'Look, there in the background! Next to the armchair.'

His parents looked at the TV, puzzled.

'Oh look, yes, they've got the same curtains as
Auntie Pauline. Isn't that nice?' said Mum.

'No! NO!' said Harry, exasperated. 'Not the
curtains! There in the corner.' He ran over and
pointed to the screen. 'They've got an electronic
bunny! That's three out of three!'

'And? Lots of people have one. So do we.'

'Exactly,' said Harry. 'Don't you think that's a
bit odd?'

'I think *you're* a bit odd,' said his mum. 'Now

finish your breakfast – you're going to be late for school.'

Jake was waiting at the corner of Crumbly Drive as usual.

'What's wrong with you?' asked Jake. 'You look like you've seen a ghost.'

'Worse than that, I've seen an electronic bunny.'

'Huh?' grunted Jake. 'What are you on about?'

'I'm not sure exactly,' said Harry. 'It's this crime wave – I just *know* they've got something to do with it.'

'You know that sounds totally insane, don't you?' said Jake, slightly concerned.

'Yeah, that's pretty much what my mum said. I dunno, it's just a feeling I have. It's . . . instinct.'

'You know what I say to that?' asked Jake.

Harry could feel a very bad joke coming.

'It *stinks*!' Jake rolled around laughing at his own joke.

'Very funny,' said Harry. 'I don't think.'

But Harry was worried. The same super soccer skills that meant he always knew where every player on the pitch was standing at any one time also meant he spotted things that nobody else did. Was he the only one who'd spotted that these bunnies were not all they seemed?

Chapter Four

Bad Bunnies

All that day at school, Harry was preoccupied. He couldn't even concentrate properly in the games lesson – he missed an open goal.

'What's the matter with you, Harry?' asked Mr Blunt. 'What about those super skills of yours?'

'Sorry, sir.'

But Harry was too busy putting together a plan. He intended to ask everybody two questions:

Did they have an electronic bunny?

Have they been burgled?

Despite it all, his team still won forty-three goals to five.

At the end of the day, Harry, Jake, Harjeet and Amy walked out of the school gate.

'Did you know,' said Harry, 'that I've talked to thirty-two people today that have electronic bunnies and over half of them have had their houses burgled – just like that woman on telly this morning. And not only that, as far as I can tell not one person has been burgled who doesn't have a bunny!'

'Oh, will you shut up about those bunnies, Harry,' said Jake. 'You've been watching too many crime programmes.'

'They're sooooo cute,' said Amy, hugging herself. 'I'm sure they couldn't be doing anything naughty, they're little kids' toys.'

'But if Harry thinks they're dodgy,' said Harjeet

unsurely, 'him being Super Soccer Boy – you know his super skills mean he notices things we don't. It's like on pitch – he can predict what the other team are going to do before they do it. My little bro has a bunny at home and I don't want all our stuff nicked.'

'Thanks!' said Harry. 'At least one of you doesn't think I'm crazy, and mark my words, they're *well* dodgy.'

Harry and Jake left the others at the bus stop and carried on home.

'Why don't you come back with me and look at Daisy's bunny?' asked Harry. 'See what you think?'

'Oh, all right then, if it will shut you up,' replied Jake, texting his mum to let her know he was going to Harry's.

Daisy thoroughly enjoyed showing off her bunny to Jake, whom she adored.

'Look, Jake, look what he can do!'

She made him talk. She made him dance. She made him sing.

She showed him how the remote control worked so that he could have a go.

'Cool! I mean, er, for a little kid's toy that is,' said Jake slightly embarrassed. 'I really can't see anything dodgy about it, Harry.'

'It's those eyes – the way they glow,' said Harry. 'They give me the creeps.'

'*You're* giving *me* the creeps,' said Jake.

37

'Anyway, I have to go, see you tomorrow. Try and chill out, Harry.'

But Harry just couldn't, and that night he found out why.

WHEEEEEEEEEEEEEEEEEEEEEE!!!!!!!!!

Harry wasn't just disturbed by unsettling dreams. He was woken up by a high-pitched, penetrating whistle, louder and more piercing than the loudest, most piercing referee's whistle he had ever heard. It got right into his skull and made his teeth vibrate. He clamped his hands tight over his ears, turned his desk lamp on with his nose and looked for something to tie around his head to muffle the sound. His ears had been super sensitive, ever since he'd been transformed into Super Soccer Boy. He could hear the speed and direction of a football, even if he couldn't see it.

'Are you OK, Ron?' Harry asked as he tied his football scarf over his ears. Even with the scarf on, the whistle was almost unbearable. Ron could obviously hear the noise and it was making his whiskers quiver, but it didn't seem to have the same effect as it did on Harry.

'It's coming from outside,' said Harry, 'somewhere up the road.'

He ran over to the window and looked up and down. The street was deserted, but then . . .

'What the . . . ?' Harry exclaimed.

The door of number twenty-two opened and out came Mr and Mrs Robinson, whose little boy was at nursery with Daisy, followed by an electronic bunny. They weren't empty handed – Mr and Mrs Robinson were carrying their plasma TV, three games consoles and a swanky-looking DVD player. Little Billy was close behind them, dragging what looked like a brand new coffee machine by its flex.

*That won't be doing
it much good,* thought
Harry absent-
mindedly as it
bumped up and
down on the uneven
stone path.

They put the
things down on the
pavement in front of
the house. Mrs
Robinson took off
her jewellery and
added it to the pile,
while Mr Robinson
went back inside and
came out with a box full of computer games and
DVDs.

Then the family just stood there. They had a
blank look about them, like they were
sleepwalking – clearly they didn't know what
they were doing.

'It must be that sound, Ron. I've got to wake them up!' Harry said.

He was just about to open his window and yell down to the street when a black van appeared from around the corner and stopped outside the Robinsons' house. Two figures, dressed in black from head to toe like ninjas, got out and loaded the Robinsons' possessions into

the van while another, the driver, walked over to
the bunny and zapped it with what looked like
a barcode scanner. The three ninjas then got
back in the van and drove slowly away.

Harry rubbed his eyes in disbelief. Then the
Robinsons slowly turned around and followed
the electronic bunny back into the house. There
was a short pause — presumably while they

locked the door and went back to bed – before the high-pitched whistle stopped abruptly and the street was silent again.

Harry was gob-smacked.

'You know what, Ron,' said Harry. 'Mum and Dad are never going to believe what we just saw. I'm going to need some hard evidence.'

Wheeeeeeee . . .!

Another whistle piped up. This time it sounded like it was a couple of streets away. From his window, Harry could see that the black

van was heading in the direction of the noise — down the hill to a street near the school. Another DIY burglary was obviously underway.

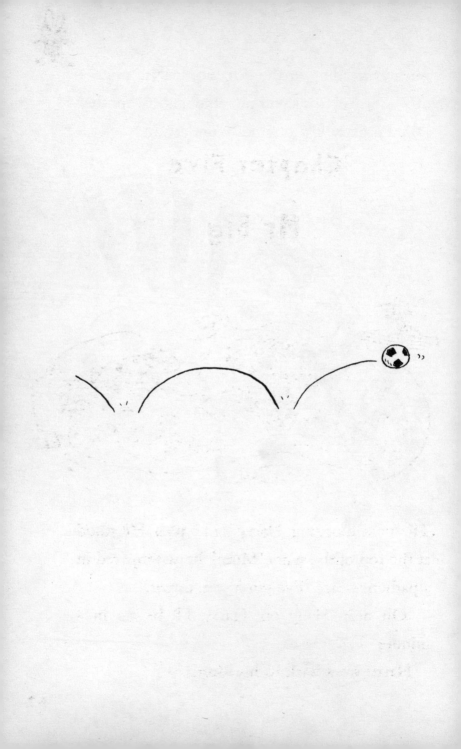

Chapter Five

Mr Big

The next morning, Harry had a plan. He stood at the top of the stairs. 'Mum!' he whimpered in a pathetic voice. 'I've got a sore throat.'

'Oh dear. Hang on, Harry, I'll be up in a minute.'

Harry went back to his room.

'OK, Ron, watch this!'

He whizzed around his room as fast as his super feet could carry him, working up quite a sweat. As soon as he heard his mum coming up the stairs, he jumped back into bed.

'Oooh, you do seem a bit hot and sweaty,' said his mum, as she felt Harry's forehead. 'And you do look a bit flushed. How do you feel?' she asked, concerned.

Cough, cough. 'Not very good,' said Harry weakly. He deserved an Oscar. 'I might be able to go to school, but I do feel a bit dizzy. Maybe I've got flu?' 'Well, you'd better stay home. I'll have to ask Mrs

Malouda from next door to pop in, though, because I have to go to work after I've taken Daisy to nursery.'

Harry knew that – it was the very reason he was pretending to be ill. His plan was to get a proper look at Daisy's bunny. He'd never get a chance normally because Daisy never let it out of her sight, but she wasn't allowed to take it to nursery. His mum went off to speak to their next door neighbour and Harry sent Jake a text to tell him what was going on.

Once the house was quiet and Harry was sure that Mrs Malouda was glued to the daytime soaps, Harry grabbed Daisy's bunny from her room and set to work.

'OK, Ron,' he said, getting out his tool kit, 'let's have a look at this baby!' He unscrewed the back of the bunny and what he found immediately rang alarm bells.

'What's this?' Harry followed a wire which

went from what seemed to be a wireless transmitter towards the back of the eye. 'It doesn't seem to be just a sensor.' He held up the bunny to the light, looking in its eyes – that was a lens there! 'This eye is a camera!' Harry said to himself. 'And if it's linked to that transmitter it means . . . that whoever made this thing can see directly into our home! This is clearly a job for Super Soccer Boy!'

Several miles away, at the headquarters (HQ) of Electronic Bunny Industries (EBI), a different sort of alarm bell was ringing.

'I have a tampering alert, Mr Codbucket, sir,' said a technician to the head of security.

'Give me the details, Miss Smythe. I'll inform Mr Big.'

Mr Big, CEO, that is Chief Executive Officer – the big boss – of Electronic Bunny Industries, was staring at his collection of toys which, rather like Daisy's, consisted mostly of bunnies.

He had toy bunnies of all shapes and sizes, in glass cases to keep them clean and germ free. He never took them out to play with – he blamed his parents for that. He blamed his parents for a lot of things.

Mr Codbucket stood in Bernard Big's massive office with the details of Harry's tampering. The office was full of electronic bunnies but these were a bigger version of the ones sold in the shops. They were Mr Big's elite force of bunnies, his own personal bodyguards.

'This could be serious, sir. The bunny is in an area that we started clearing last night. It could be that someone is suspicious.'

'I doubt it,' said Mr Big dismissively. 'Anyway, how would they avoid the sonic mind control? It's probably just some annoying brat playing with a screwdriver. It'll be back together by this afternoon – that is if it doesn't end up in the bin. Is the transmitter still active?'

'Yes, sir,' said Codbucket, nodding.

'Well, it's not a problem then, is it? Switch the bunny to full surveillance mode and let me know of any further developments. We may as well clear that area tonight anyway. See to it, Codbucket.'

Mr Big turned to his computer screen and looked at the electronic bunny sales figures.

'These things are making me a fortune! What

with that and my little sideline, heh, heh, I'll soon be the richest man on the planet. And then comes the next part of the plan. My bunnies and I will take over the world!'

All of the bunnies in the room turned in unison to Mr Big. Their huge eyes flashed menacingly and their nylon whiskers twitched and quivered. It was an awesome sight.

Back in Crumbly Drive, Harry was trying to work out what to say to his mum. 'She's going to be so mad at me for messing about with Daisy's bunny, Ron, but I have to show her what I've found.'

When his mum got home a couple of hours later she was, as Harry had expected, very cross.

'I'm *so* mad at you for messing about with Daisy's bunny!' she said. 'What were you thinking?'

'But Mum, look at the camera and the transmitter and . . . I think they send out some sort of sonic wave that controls people's brains. It's the bunnies who are behind the burglaries!'

'But nothing, Harry. You're being totally ridiculous. This fever has obviously affected your brain. Now, you'd better put that bunny back

together exactly how it was before Daisy sees it
or you're grounded for a month!'

'OK, Mum,' said Harry miserably.

Harry did as he was told, but while he was
working, he decided it would be a good idea to
make himself a pair of earplugs to filter out the
bunnies' whistle, just in case.

Before long, the bunny was as good as new (or
bad as new, depending on your point of view) and
the earplugs were ready. He stood the bunny on
his desk and stared at it. The bunny stared back.

On the other side of town at the HQ of EBI, Miss Smythe was still on duty. She looked at the image that was being transmitted by Daisy's bunny.

'Wait a moment,' she said slowly. 'I'm sure I recognise that boy.'

SECTION 3

Chapter Six

Mind Control

That night Harry was woken again by the high-pitched whistle, but this time he was prepared. He put in the earplugs he'd made and, although it still felt like his teeth were being drilled, the horrible high-pitched whistle was just about bearable. He looked out of his bedroom window.

'Oh no, Ron!' he shouted. 'It's *our* house! Mum, Dad and Daisy are burgling our own house! I have to stop them.' He ran to his bedroom door.

'It won't open. But it can't be locked – there's no key.' He squinted through the keyhole and saw that something was wedged against his door – there was no way he could get out. 'The window!' said Harry. 'I think I'm going to need my utility boots, Ron, and I think you'd better stay here.' His utility boots were the special football boots he'd designed and built just for occasions like this.

Harry climbed on to his windowsill and, with his boots in hover mode, he descended into the

front garden, landing right next to Mum, Dad and Daisy.

'WAKE UP! WAKE UP!' he yelled, jumping up and down in front of them like a maniac. They didn't even twitch.

Harry looked up and down his road.

Lots of people were coming out of their houses and dumping their possessions in the street. Harry zoomed up and down trying to get his neighbours to wake from their trances. He shouted at them, ran around them, even shook them, but nothing worked. It seemed that he really was the only one unaffected by the sound.

And as more bunnies emerged the louder the whistling sound became.

He picked up one of the bunnies and shook it roughly. 'Stop it you EVIL LITTLE BUNNY! STOP IT!'

Instantly its eyes lit up and flashed threateningly – sparks came from its whiskers and Harry dropped it, feeling like he'd had an electric shock.

He looked over his shoulder, back towards his house. The street was lined with electronic bunnies, their evil eyes glinting in the moonlight. They moved towards him to form a wall, several bunnies deep, between him and his house. They may have been small but he would rather have faced any wall of players on a pitch than face these evil little bunnies.

Harry was seriously spooked. There was nothing else for it. 'GERONIMO!' Harry yelled as he bolted, booting the bunnies left, right and centre with his most powerful super soccer kicks as he went.

THWACK! WHACK! They went flying. Unfortunately one of them flew straight through someone's front window.

'Get!' *Boot.* 'Out!' *Boot.* 'OF MY WAY!' *Boot.*

Harry sped back towards his own house. He picked up their PS3 and Wii and crept inside the house just before a black van stopped outside. It

was all he could save though – by the time he went back outside, everything else had been loaded into the van and Daisy's bunny was being zapped with the scanner.

'Hey!' said the ninja doing the scanning. 'This is the bunny that had been tampered with.' He looked up, not quite fast enough to see Harry flatten himself against the wall.

'OK,' said another, 'I've made a note of the address.'

Harry felt a cold shiver of foreboding trickle down his spine. *I don't like the sound of that,* he thought. Harry's mum, dad and sister turned and walked up the garden path and into the house. Harry watched while his mum locked the door, then she and his sister went to bed while his dad removed the large chest which he had pushed in front of Harry's door. Wearily, Harry went back to his bedroom. The whistling sound ceased and everything was quiet again.

'What am I going to do, Ron?' said Harry, collapsing on the bed exhausted, and he fell asleep immediately, still wearing his boots.

Chapter Seven

A Nasty Surprise

EEEEEEEEEKK!

Harry was woken by a different sound – his mum's loud scream.

'Oh no!'

He heard his dad rush downstairs to see what was going on.

'Here goes, Ron ... Maybe now it's happened to us they'll listen to me. I'd better tell them what I saw.' He ran down and found his parents in the living room.

'It's exactly what happened to the Robinsons,' wailed Mum, 'except they didn't take our games

consoles. Already stolen plenty, I suppose.'

'No, actually, that was me,' said Harry brightly. Then he described the previous night's events to his parents as they stood open-mouthed. You could have heard a pin drop. '. . . So you see, I was right all along – it's the electronic bunnies.'

Mr and Mrs Gribble looked at each other. Mrs Gribble burst into tears.

'This isn't a joke, Harry,' said Dad in a I-hope-you're-listening-because-I-really-mean-this voice.

'I *know*, Dad. We have to do something.'

'Maybe that lightning did something to his brain. Maybe he needs a doctor,' Mum wailed. 'Maybe it's my fault – I'm probably spending too much time with Daisy.'

'*Muuum!*'

'Don't worry, dear.' Mr Gribble put his arm around his wife. 'It was probably just a bad dream because of the fever.'

'BUT I DON'T HAVE A FEVER!' yelled Harry. 'I never —'

'Well, off you go and get ready for school then while Mum and I ring the police,' said Mr Gribble, getting cross.

'Good luck with that,' said Harry. 'Half the street was raided last night – they'll be very busy.' Harry glanced down. 'Anyway, if it was all a dream then why am I still wearing my utility boots?'

They looked at Harry's feet.

'To be honest, Harry, you're *always* wearing football boots,' said Mum.

'But not these!'

'School!' bellowed Dad.

Harry was exasperated. 'But —'

'HARRY!' they said in unison.

That was it. Harry knew that when they both said his name together like that he was wasting his breath. He was on his own. Or was he?

'Mum,' he said from halfway up the stairs, 'can Jake sleep over tonight? It's Friday anyway and we can go to football practice together in the morning.'

'If it will stop you going on about this ridiculous bunny business, then yes,' she said wearily.

'Thanks, Mum.' *Now all I have to do is convince Jake that I'm not crazy*, Harry thought to himself.

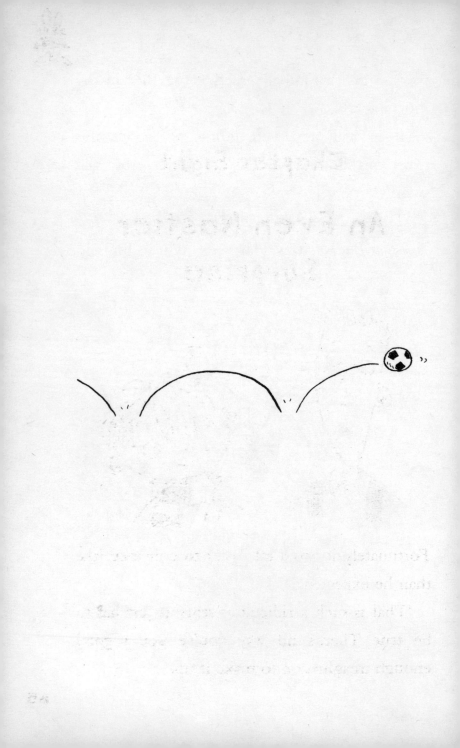

Chapter Eight

An Even Nastier Surprise

Fortunately, it was a lot easier to convince Jake than he expected.

'That is such a ridiculous story it just has to be true. There's no way you've got a good enough imagination to make it up.'

'Er, thanks, I think,' said Harry.

He showed Jake the earplugs. 'That whistling seems to come from each electronic bunny. It seems to cause some sort of mind control. It doesn't work on me though, it just hurts like crazy so I made these.'

'Awesome! I could do with a pair of these when my mum and dad play Singstar.'

'I've made you a pair already. You'll need them tonight.'

'O . . . K . . . So why am I now feeling just a teensy bit worried?' asked Jake.

'Well, the plan is you sleep over at my place and you wear the earplugs so that they block you from the mind control. Then, you and I sneak into one of the black vans and find out where the stuff is being taken to,' said Harry.

'Right. Well, that sounds nice and dangerous. Then what?' Jake asked, getting more nervous by the second.

'I'll have to work that out when we get to wherever the van goes. I guess we just need to get evidence to show the police.'

'Great plan,' Jake said, sarcastically.

'Got a better one?' Harry asked.

At EBI HQ, a meeting was underway in Mr Big's office.

'We have a problem, sir,' said Mr Codbucket. 'What you see here is footage captured by the BunnyCams. It looks like we're dealing with a young boy called Harry Gribble, who also goes by the name of Super Soccer Boy.'

'Hmmmm. What a nasty little fly in the ointment. Clearly we need to thwart whatever plan he's hatching.' Mr Big looked up at the ceiling, lost in thought. He looked around at his bunny bodyguards and smiled evilly.

'Codbucket!'

'Yes, sir.'

'This is what I want you to do . . .'

At 49 Crumbly Drive, Harry and Jake had just finished stuffing their faces with pizza – extra

hot jalapenos for Harry, Hawaiian for Jake. They played keepy-uppy in the garden for ages before settling down for the night. Normally they would have played on the PS3 or the Wii too but of course the TV was gone.

'I hope this will be OK,' said Jake nervously.

'It'll be fine, trust me,' said Harry putting on his Super Soccer Boy utility boots and cape in readiness, and handing Jake a set of earplugs. But he didn't exactly feel super confident himself.

'What about your earplugs?' asked Jake.

'I'll put mine in when the bunnies wake me up.' *If I can get to sleep in the first place*, he thought.

Sleep wasn't a problem though. Not long after he turned off the light, Jake started to snore softly and, pretty soon, Harry had dropped off too.

A few hours later, Harry was woken once more by the horrible whistling, though it seemed even louder that night. Ron was standing on his chest, trying to wake him up. Harry shoved in his earplugs, shook Jake awake and groped for the light.

When the light went on, Harry and Jake froze. The room was full of evil electronic bunnies! But these bunnies were different – they were bigger and more menacing. Harry's plan had been to stow away in a black van – he'd never expected the bunnies to come to him!

Harry and Jake were bound and gagged, taken downstairs, bundled into a van and driven off at high speed back to Bunny HQ, Ron hanging on desperately to Harry's cape.

Chapter Nine

Mr Big's Evil Plans

'Well then, what do we have here?' said Mr Big leaning over his massive desk in his massive office. Harry and Jake stood on the other side.

Jake was white as a sheet and was trying hard not to throw up. All he could think of was the half digested Hawaiian pizza bubbling away in his belly. The Bunny Guards surrounded them, standing to attention.

'It seems to me,' Mr Big continued, getting up and towering over the two small boys, 'that you've got yourselves into a bit of a pickle.'

Mr Big was so large and wide that Harry began to wonder if Mr Big was his real name or just a nickname.

'You won't get away with this!' shouted Harry defiantly. 'They'll be looking for us.'

'Oh, don't worry,' smiled Mr Big. 'You'll be back home by morning. No one will ever know that you were gone. It's just that you'll be . . . how should I put it? A little different?!'

Jake looked at Harry with an expression that said, *What have you got me into now?*

'Why are you doing this?' asked Harry. 'You're just a common thief.'

'Oh no, not at all,' boomed Mr Big. 'The electronic bunny burglaries are just the first part of my plan. Let me explain – I might as well because you won't remember any of it later!'

Jake gulped down a sicky burp.

'I'll show you my Powerpoint presentation. It explains it all beautifully.'

Phase One - The Electronic Bunnies Hit the Shops

- Everybody wants one of these adorable little playmates.

- The BunnyCams spy on the family sending back details to Bunny HQ.

- Bunny Mind Control Ray is transmitted to bunny households.

- Owners deposit their possessions outside to be collected by ninjas.

'This is what you know so far, but there is so much more!'

Phase Two - Very Nearly New

- We open a new chain of second-hand shops called 'Very Nearly New', great for those wanting a bargain.

- Goods collected by ninjas are sorted and distributed all over country after security markings and serial numbers are changed.

- Goods are re-sold (some to those who have 'donated' to us!).

- Bunnies do their work once more.

'It's perfect! Recycling at its very best. Mwahahahaha!' Mr Big jumped up and down like an excited schoolgirl. 'I hope you're enjoying the show, children. THERE'S SO MUCH MORE!'

Phase Three – WORLD DOMINATION!!

✓ **Establish effectiveness of sonic mind control ray.**

✓ **Research and development of mind ray to re-programme the brain.**

○ **Test on human subjects.**

○ **Go national.**

○ **Take over the world.**

Harry and Jake gaped in amazement.

'I can see you're impressed,' said Mr Big smugly. 'It's a sort of brain-washing but I like to call it bunny-washing! Ha ha, ha ha ha ha ...' Mr Big laughed in a high-pitched squeally sort of way, like someone who is slightly unhinged.

'You're mad!' said Harry.

'Hmmm, no, I don't think so, just a mild personality disorder, I suspect. Anyway, as you can see, on my World Domination list only the first two checkboxes are ticked. As yet, we haven't tried our new ray on a human subject, but now you've kindly volunteered, we can surge ahead. For that, boys, I am most deeply grateful.' He bowed, humbly. 'Now, my little

bunnies, take them down to the repair shop and lock them in while we prepare the experiment. See you in an hour or so, boys. Ta ta!'

Harry and Jake were led away. Jake was close to tears.

'Don't worry, Jake, I'll think of something,' Harry whispered.

Jake made a feeble attempt at a smile and sniffed miserably.

Chapter Ten

A Remote Chance

Harry and Jake were taken by the Bunny Guard and locked in a large room that was full of bits and pieces of bunnies. There were also some whole bunnies, lined up on a bench in various states of repair. The shelves were full of boxes containing spare parts and the walls were papered with cutaway pictures, wiring diagrams and repair schedules.

Harry immediately set Ron down on one of the worktops and started searching for something to help them escape.

Jake searched for something to be sick in – the queasy feeling had *not* gone away.

'I hope you have a plan,' said Jake shakily, 'because as far as I can see, we're done for.'

'I'm working on it,' answered Harry, looking through the boxes of spare parts for inspiration.

'They're watching everything you do, you know,' said Jake, pointing to a CCTV camera high in the corner of the room.

'That's easy,' said Harry. He picked up a bottle of machine oil, aimed at the lens with his Super Soccer Boy super-accurate aim and squirted.

'SHOT!' cried Jake.

'Ron, climb up and spread the oil over the lens – it'll make their picture all blurry,' said Harry.

Ron did as instructed and Jake cheered up a bit.

Harry looked around the windowless room.

'Well, obviously we can't get out of a window . . . and there are too many bunnies to fight just by ourselves . . .'

'Those bigger ones are really freaky. Their eyes sort of flash and they buzz all the time,' said Jake.

'Hmmm, yes,' said Harry not really listening. 'If only we could disable them somehow.'

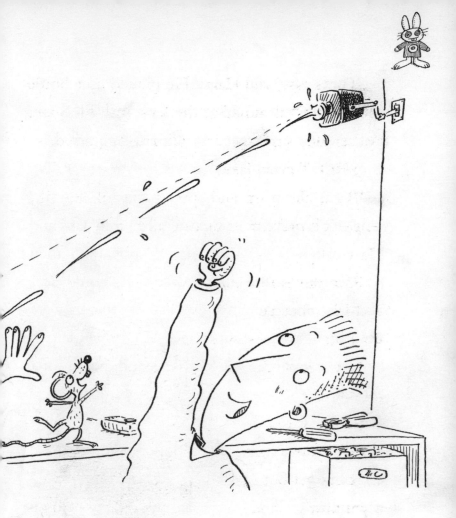

'Yes?' said Jake encouragingly.

'Got it!' said Harry so suddenly it made Jake jump. Mind you, almost anything would have made him jump at this point in time.

'SOUNDWAVES!' shouted Harry, grabbing Jake by the shoulders and staring wildly.

'Huh?' Jake said, puzzled.

'No time to explain now. Quick, hand me that box of remote controls and one of those bunnies while I clear myself a workspace. We don't have long.'

Harry worked at a feverish pace while Jake and Ron watched nervously. Every now and then Jake listened at the door to see if he could hear anyone coming to get them. Harry's fingers were a blur as he used his super speed to dismantle two remote controls, re-wired things and did all sorts of weird stuff that Jake didn't understand, until . . .

'There. Finished . . . I think.' Harry held up two remote controls. 'The question is, have we got time to test them?'

'Dare I ask what they're supposed to

do?' Jake asked anxiously.

'Well, what I've done, in simple terms, is re-calibrate the dynamic force of the sonic mind-control transmitter and reverse its focus to make it an . . .'

'Whoa, stop. *Simple* terms, Harry, we don't

all have Super Soccer Boy brains like you.'

'Sorry . . . Well, basically, I've adapted the remote controls to reverse the sonic mind-control wave so that the bunnies send it to themselves, and I've made the signal stronger so that it messes with their control systems. At least, it *should* do, but I can't be sure until we've tried them.'

'But what will that do?' asked Jake. 'Why —'

They both turned as they heard the door being unlocked.

'Looks like we're trying them right now,' said Jake.

Harry threw him a controller as the door flew open. Four bunny guards moved into the room.

'Press the red button and point it at the bunnies,' Harry yelled quickly.

The effect was instantaneous. The two at the front stopped dead. Their eyes flashed wildly and they began to rock from side to side. Little sparks came off their whiskers and they began to make a strange whirring sound.

Then suddenly they began to spin really fast, first of all just where they stood, but then all around the room, bouncing off the walls and knocking things over. By this time the other two had started to spin. It was getting pretty dangerous.

WHIRRR! WHIRRR! WHIRRR!

'Quick, we'd better get out of the way,' said
Harry, grabbing Jake and Ron and weaving his
way to the door. Just in time in fact – the first two
bunnies stopped spinning suddenly, they stood

completely still for a moment or two and then their heads blew clean off, creating a shower of sparks, computer components and nuts and bolts.

'I think, Harry, you could safely say that your remotes work,' Jake said, grinning. 'That was awesome!'

They ran down the corridor leaving the other two bunnies spinning out of control after them.

However, Codbucket had been watching the whole thing on the Bunny Guards' BunnyCam.

'They've done something to the bunnies and

escaped, sir. They're in the corridor near the repair room.'

'That's OK, we're ready for them. All the doors except the lab door are locked, aren't they?' asked Mr Big.

'Yes, sir.'

'Well, that's the only place they can go then. Meet me down there. This should be fun!' he said with an evil grin.

Chapter Eleven

The Brain-Washer

The door to the staircase was locked, so Harry and Jake ran down the corridor trying every door as they went.

'This one's unlocked!' said Jake excitedly, and before Harry had a chance to stop him, he went inside. Harry had no choice but to follow. The

door slammed behind him and Harry saw Mr Big, who'd made his own way to the lab through a passageway from his office. He had Jake in an armlock!

'I'll take those, I think,' he said, pushing Jake towards Harry and snatching their remote controls. He put them on top of a filing cabinet out of their reach and several of the bunnies surrounded it. 'Very clever you are, young man, but not quite clever enough.'

Codbucket joined them in the lab with the rest of the bunnies.

Harry spotted a large machine in the corner of the room. It was built around the kind of chair that you get at a dentist's. A large helmet with lights and wires attached to it was suspended over the head end. There was what looked like a control panel on the brain-washing machine and in the middle of it was a dial with various settings:

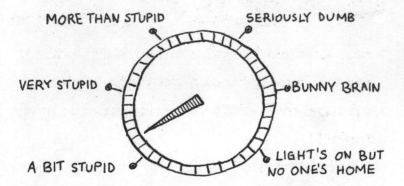

'I can see you're admiring my lovely machine. She's a beauty, isn't she? And just think, you're about to be the first to try it. What an honour!'

Mr Big strolled over and switched it on. It hummed into life. The bunnies swayed from side to side in rhythm to the hum.

'Well, it's been fun, young Gribble, but time is pressing and we need to get you back home, so if you'd be kind enough to come with me.' He stepped towards Harry meaning to take him over to the chair.

SUPER CRRRUNNCH!

But Harry wasn't going quietly. He kicked Mr
Big super hard in the shin.

CRUNCH!

'OWWW!' yelled Mr Big in agony. 'Not fair!
Get him, bunnies!'

The bunnies all went for Harry at once.

'Quick, Ron, get the remotes!'

Ron leapt off Harry's shoulder and scampered
around the room while Harry dived and dodged
the bunnies as if they were trying to tackle him.

But there were
far too many.
Jake, frozen by fear until
now, ran over and kicked
Mr Big, a little feebly, in
the other shin. But Harry
had spotted Codbucket
who was going for
the remotes.
'Jake! Stop Codbucket!'

'Oh no you don't!' yelled Jake going for a
tackle. But Codbucket was stronger than he
looked and Jake was just dragged across the
floor. There was only one thing he could do. He
bit Codbucket hard on the ankle.

'OWWW!' screamed Codbucket.

Now both men were hopping around the room!

Ron had reached the remote controls and
began to push them off the filing cabinet.

Harry did the most fantastic goal-keeper's
leap to catch the remotes. He pressed the button
and threw the other remote to Jake.

'Quick, Jake. Catch!' called Harry.

They pressed the buttons at the same time and the bunnies froze.

Their eyes flashed alarmingly.

Their whiskers twitched and crackled.

They started to spin.

'Oh no! My bunnies!' wailed Mr Big as he stumbled towards his machine. 'Not my lovely bunnies!' He plonked himself down in the chair

blubbing and rubbing his shins just as the first bunny's head blew off. Harry intercepted it and kicked it with perfect accuracy at the helmet, which dropped on to Mr Big's head with a plop.

'What?! What's going on?' Mr Big exclaimed, groping around, unable to see. He knocked the dial on the control panel with his elbow on to the setting which said *Bunny Brain*. Before they knew what was happening, another bunny exploded and a rather large bolt shot straight towards the *Go* switch.

'Ooops!' said Harry. 'Oh dear,' said Jake, backing away from the machine as it started whirring loudly. 'Mr Big!' shouted Codbucket. Ron just squeaked. The machine vibrated slightly and Mr Big's large body went limp. It all happened very quickly and despite Codbucket's attempts to fight his way through the bits of flying bunny, there was nothing anyone could do. Mr Big's expression changed from one of surprise to one of complete blankness. Then his nose began to twitch.

One by one, the rest of the bunnies each met their grisly end. It was like a war zone. Then, somewhere in the building, a siren began to sound.

'We need to get out of here,' Harry said to Jake

as he rescued Ron from the midst of the massacre. 'Codbucket, let us out of this building before you end up like your boss.'

Codbucket was too shocked to argue. He pushed a code into a panel by the door. 'I've disabled all the locks. You're free to go,' he said miserably.

The last they saw of Mr Big, the large man was doing a very good impersonation of a sweet little bunny – twitchy nose, bunny teeth and all.

'Let's head for home, Jake,' said Harry.

'What about the police?'

'Oh, I think that can wait until the morning,' replied Harry, yawning and stretching. 'I'm too tired for explanations right now.'

Explanations, however, were the last thing on either of their minds when they came out of the front of Electronic Bunny Industries.

'Oh dear,' said Harry.

It looked as if all the electronic bunnies in existence were making their way to HQ: every centimetre of the forecourt was already packed with bunnies. The streets outside were filling up too. Harry wondered if Daisy's bunny was on its way or whether it would be too far away to be affected by the siren.

They did not look like happy bunnies. Hundreds of flashing eyes turned towards Harry and Jake. Hundreds of nylon whiskers twitched and crackled.

'I wondered what that siren was about. It must have been calling the bunnies,' said Harry. He pointed to the large metal gate opposite.

'Stay close behind me, and keep pressing the remote control buttons,' he said. Harry stepped slowly into the crowd. 'OK, one, two, three . . . GO!'

Harry sped forward, kicking as he went, while Jake did his best to keep up, clicking the remote controls at each bunny. At last, the first bunnies started to spin. Everywhere they looked, there were bunnies twitching and sparking out of control.

'Ow!' said Harry as an exploding head showered him with sparks. 'Let's get out of here before we get pulverised by bunny bits.'

As they came out of the gates, more bunnies were still coming, filling the streets, but they were already going haywire.

'Looks like we've set off a chain reaction,' said Harry, ducking a piece of circuit board. 'We need to get off the streets!'

Harry gave Jake a piggyback and headed back to his house at super speed.

As they drew closer to home they saw that most of the bunnies had already met their fate and Harry and Jake were able to walk safely. The rest of the country was waking up to streets full of headless bunnies. It was quite a sight.

Chapter Twelve

Man of the Match

When they reached Harry's house, the first thing they heard was the sound of Daisy crying her eyes out.

'MY BUNNNNNYYYY! Boo hoo. I want BUNNY!'

Mrs Gribble was rather surprised to see Harry and Jake walk in the front door.

'You're up early,' she said.

'Harry. [*Sniff sniff*.] Look at my BUNNY!' howled Daisy. 'He's all broke.'

There in the corner was Daisy's bunny, smoking gently.

'Yes I know, Daisy,' said Harry, in a very sympathetic voice considering what he'd been through. 'They all are.'

'You've heard then,' said his mum. 'It's really weird. There was a newsflash on TV warning everyone to be careful. Apparently there's been some sort of major malfunction. Not one bunny has survived.'

'Phew,' said Harry under his breath.

Jake hid the remote controls behind his back.

Harry picked up the broken bunny and collected up the bits he could find. 'Let me see if I can help him,' he said kindly.

'Oh, could you try?' said Mum. 'That would be lovely! I'll make you and Jake some breakfast.'

'Anything but carrots,' Harry whispered to his friend.

'How about a fry up?'

133

'Thanks, Mrs G,' said Jake, instantly regaining his appetite.

They plodded upstairs and without an awful lot of difficulty, Harry put Daisy's bunny back together leaving out, of course, a certain sonic mind-control transmitter, just in case. The bunny had a few scorch marks, but it looked pretty good.

'Here you are, Daisy,' he said taking it back downstairs. '*Almost* as good as new.'

Daisy was so happy she nearly burst. She ran
over and covered him in sloppy kisses.

'I luv you, big Harry!' she said, teary-eyed.

'YUK!' said Harry.

HARRY'S FOOTBALL FACTS!

The Greeks used inflated pigs bladders to play football.

The chelsea goalkeeper in 1905-1906 was William 'fatty' Foulkes. He weighed over 22 stone, that's 140kg! (He ate all the pies!)

Over 32 billion people watch the world cup on tv.

The fastest ever international goal was scored in 8.3 seconds by San Marino against England on Nov 17th 1993.

GOAL!!! GOAL!?

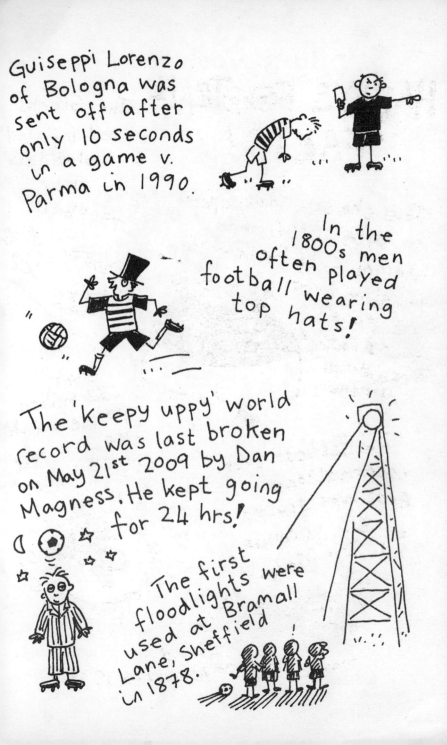

Guiseppi Lorenzo of Bologna was sent off after only 10 seconds in a game v. Parma in 1990.

In the 1800s men often played football wearing top hats!

The 'keepy uppy' world record was last broken on May 21st 2009 by Dan Magness. He kept going for 24 hrs!

The first floodlights were used at Bramall Lane, Sheffield in 1878.

Have you read . . .

Harry really loves football. It's just a shame he is so useless at it! But one day, as he watches footie on TV, a bolt of lightning hits the house, and something really peculiar happens. The next time Harry practises his kicks, he finds he can control the ball like a pro! He has become . . . SUPER SOCCER BOY!

It's not long before Super Soccer Boy has to use all his skills to solve a strange case of exploding footballs!

Coming soon . . . .

Super Soccer Boy and the Snot Monsters

Everybody in Middletown seems to have a cold. Professor Mucus says he's looking for a cure, but Harry's super senses tell him there's something shifty about the scientist. Will Harry discover what he's really up to?

Super Soccer Boy and the Attack of the Giant Slugs

A chemical spill turns hundreds of slugs into giants bent on revenge. How is Harry ever going to stop the slimy maniacs?

Join
Super Soccer Boy
online:

www.supersoccerboy.com

⚽Fun activities
⚽Football facts and quiz
⚽All the latest on the books

And much more!